MOM

One Life to Live?
Maybe Not.

STEPHEN ZACK

Copyright @ 2012 by Stephen Zack.

All rights reserved. No part of this publication may be reproduced, distributed, or transmitted in any form or by any means without the written permission of the author.

Inquiries can be directed to the author at stephenzackauthor@comcast.net.

ISBN 978-0-9885006-0-0

Printed in the United States of America.

To

MOM

(Who else?)

I

I'LL NEVER FORGET THE DAY MOM CAME HOME.

It was a Friday morning, and I finally was getting ready to go back to work, thinking again how Mom would've loved her funeral, there'd been so many good things to eat afterwards. Then, for the better part of a week, the four maiden aunts who fill out our overfed family in more ways than one had sent me casseroles and cakes. To keep my spirits up, they said. Actually, my spirits hadn't been so high in months, though my gut was starting to sag. A family trait, I guess. I'd become a connoisseur of condolence cooking – hearty, high calorie peasant fare meant to be eaten during a long Eastern European winter. Comfort food. The kind of food that makes you feel fine "regardless..." And I'd been feeling fine to begin with.

At last, Mom was gone.

I was tearing into some delicious apple cake (Mom never would've let me eat cake for breakfast) when the doorbell rang. I waddled to the door wondering who it could be at that early hour, reminding myself the extra pounds I'd gained weren't going to do anything good for my sex life. Whoever it was, I hoped they wouldn't stay long. After three days spent settling Mom's affairs *post mortem*, I had to be getting to my workshop. It wasn't that my inventions would be suffering without me; I *wanted* nothing more than to get back into the swing of things. Except for the weight of too many foods fried without Crisco, there was spring in my step again.

Now that Mom was dead, I felt alive.

Eighteen months ago, I'd given up life as I knew it to move in with her. Once Mom got sick she needed somebody to take care of her. Lucky me, the only child. You'd think someone else could've taken her for a while, what with four unoccupied old maids around, the sum total of our living blood relations. *But no-o.* I had to give up an apartment in the city, a studio apartment in a high-rise near my shop where I was living the life of a content, confirmed bachelor still young enough at thirty-two to have a good time. Mom hadn't approved of the lifestyle. She used to wag her finger at me and say:

"Don't become an old bachelor...all old bachelors are peculiar."

She should've known peculiar.

MOM

I moved a curtain to look out a window the way Mom always used to do. A white truck was parked in front of the house, a big moving van type of rig that brushed low branches of the trees, still leafless in the last weeks of winter, that lined our quiet street. The truck had what looked like a refrigerator unit on top, whirring away. No markings.

I have to admit it'd been better for Mom when she was sick to be at home in the burbs where she grew up and where her sisters lived, even if they never did much besides visit and gossip on the phone with her. I could commute all right to my workshop. Who said you can't go home again? Despite the hour-long drive each way in rush-hour traffic to an industrial park on the outskirts of Newark, it wasn't too bad until the last six months when Mom was dying. The last six months were hell, watching her waste away and not be able to do anything about it. I don't even like to think about that. I had to spend most of my time with her then. I'd been the dutiful son. But I missed having my own place, missed the lights of the city, the view across rooftops, the anonymity of numbers that lets you do anything you want. That bachelor pad, tiny and awfully expensive, was worth every penny for the sake of my social life alone. With

Mom gone, I figured I'd sell the old homestead and maybe buy a condo at the shore. Women like that kind of thing. Summer was a long way off, but already I was dreaming of sleek young bodies, tanning in the sun...

The guy I saw outside ringing the bell – leaning on it – wore a long white lab coat, open and flapping in the breeze. He was a little guy, kind of pear-shaped, reading a clipboard through glasses that were so thick his googly eyes looked like those of a fresh caught bass. He had on khaki pants as creased as a pair of concertinas, a blue shirt he must've slept in, and the last clip-on tie in captivity. A plastic pen holder advertising some prescription drug bulged with cheap Bics in a front pocket, giving him a chesty appearance. The comb-over from one side of his bald, round head to the other completed the nerdy image. I opened the door expecting to learn he'd stopped at the wrong house to make a delivery or something. I planned to get rid of him fast and take off.

In a foreign voice that made him sound like a professorial Arnold Schwarzenegger, he asked:

"Is this the Kravath *Residenz?*"

"Yeah."

"And you are..." he looked at the clipboard, "Stefan Kravath?"

MOM

"Steve Kravath, yeah…"

"We are from the Institute."

"Yeah?"

So long as I was there, Mom had been able to stay at home, as she wanted to, and have her sisters visit almost to the end. When she felt the end was near she had herself taken by ambulance to the "Eterna Institute" in upstate New York. It was all pre-arranged; she never discussed it much with me. I only knew the Institute was like a hospice where they did medical research and organ transplants, or something. Mom supported all that organ donor stuff, I'd supposed, in the hope of having a part of her live on after death in somebody else's body cavity. She always was into weird. I talked her out of being cryogenically frozen (too iffy) so I figured I had to humor her in this. Toward the end I thought she was losing it, anyway. I didn't look around much or ask many questions the one time I visited the Institute, just before she died. I should have. I should've before Mom – or what was left of her after organ removal – arrived at the mortuary for the funeral. She'd insisted on having a closed casket. Because so much would be missing? I wondered if that was why the undertaker stared at me strangely all through the service.

The funny looking guy standing on the stoop now made the slightest sign toward the truck and a hatch in the side popped open like a door on a spaceship. Before I knew what was happening, he handed me a business card and brushed past into the house. The card read:

Hugo Haupt, Ph.D., Eterna Institute

I nearly was knocked down by two jump-suited technicians who followed wheeling between them what looked to be a lamp of some sort. I say the thing looked like a lamp, but it really was unrecognizable, just a rectangular steel box about the size and shape of an ordinary clothes hamper, painted black with a satin finish and surmounted by a large, white glass globe. I guess the globe reminded me of the lamps that were trendy back in the sixties. And I could see outlets at the base of the box for electrical connections. So I thought it was a lamp. They went right to the front room with it.

"Excuse me..." I said, trying to get an explanation, *"Excu-u-use me..."* (doing my best Steve Martin impression). But they paid no attention. They moved the TV chair that's always been at one end of the room. There they put the lamp thing on a chrome stand, raising it another half foot up off the floor. *Wait a minute!*

MOM

That chair was the only comfortable one in the room. You could sit back in it and watch the big-screen TV (Mom loved TV) or look out the picture window and see the whole length of Oak Street. Mom loved Oak Street, too. They were upsetting everything. But I calmed myself; after the Eterna people left, I figured I could move the lamp and put the chair back where it belonged.

A whole troop of technicians spilled from the van like Shriners piling out of a Volkswagen. They slipped soundlessly around the house, congregating especially in the basement. They all seemed identical, as alien and silent as Captain Nemo's crew in the movie *"Twenty Thousand Leagues Under the Sea."* They carried cords and hauled hoses and began drilling through the living room floor down into the furnace room. Drilling – that was too much!

"Uh...Dr. Haupt..."

"Call me Hugo," he said (pronouncing it *HOO-go*).

"What's going on here?"

"You do not know?" He acted as if everything ought to be self-evident. "It was arranged..."

"Well, bring me up to date on the details before you continue, okay?"

The work never stopped. Without saying anything more, Hugo walked over to the lamp and, with both hands, carefully started to unscrew the heavy glass globe. He turned it around one complete revolution, then lifted straight up, gently.

What I took as a likeness of Mom's head, bald as a billiard ball, was affixed to the top of the black box. Without much neck and tilted back slightly, it made me think of a Halloween jack-o'-lantern. The head was a pretty good copy, I thought, though a little waxy and without much color. To tell the truth, it looked better than Mom had toward the end. I assumed it was a gift in appreciation for giving her all to the Institute. I could tell Hugo was waiting for me to comment, so I tried to be complimentary:

"It...it looks just like her."

"Ja, natürlich," he replied (a little testily, I felt). "It should...it *is* her!"

I thought, that's disgusting! But I kept it to myself and said, "You mean she's actually stuffed and mounted...like a big game trophy?"

He almost dropped his clipboard.

You really do not understand, do you?"

The tone suggested he wanted to add "...poor boy," out of pity for my ignorance.

MOM

"Mrs. Kravath – your mother – is alive!"

"Alive?" I stared at Mom. I never thought I'd see her again; not here, in the front room, anyway.

"She is in a state of suspended animation now, but we are going to revivify her," Hugo said as matter-of-factly as Werner von Braun talking about a moon shot *circa* 1950 (when everyone *knew* it was impossible). "It will take several hours because we have a lot of infrastructure to install." Someone came in to connect a conduit to the base of the box.

"That's Mom?" I still couldn't believe it. "In that box?"

"No. No..." He obviously thought I was an imbecile. "Only her head and neck exist now. The black box is a portable life support module."

"Oh?" I should've known that?

"The important thing is...the brain – *the mind* – lives!"

Hugo fairly frothed. His eyebrows arched and, behind those thick glasses, his fishy eyes glowed. I was uncomfortably reminded of the "lights of perverted science" that Winston Churchill used to orate about. I saw that Mom's eyes were closed.

"Are you sure you can revive her?"

"We have done it in the lab already," the little geek assured me smugly.

Faltering, I said, "I was on my way to work…" I started thinking now that I really ought to stay.

"Go. Go…we will take care of *every*-thing," he spoke as if to a child. "We will not bring her around until you come back, I promise…"

"I'll just put in half a day…" I said.

Actually, I wanted to make a few phone calls.

"Do not worry…be happy!" he said.

I had a very bad feeling. But I left.

I drove all the way out to my workshop to give myself time to think and to have a place where I could talk in privacy. At the workshop, I got on the phone right away. I called an old friend, a guy I'd gone to high school with who's a big-time neurosurgeon at a med school in New York now. Mike knows all about research. After tossing him a quick, "How's the wife? How's the girlfriend?" I asked, trying to sound casual:

"Uh, what do you know about the Eterna Institute?"

He waxed so enthusiastic I was taken off balance. He said the Institute is "on the cutting edge" of medical technology, that they do a lot of "exciting" experimental research there.

"Exciting, huh?"

"Why're you interested?"

"Oh...Mom donated her organs to the Institute," I said, trying not to give anything away. "I wanted to make sure the place is legit."

He laughed, "Don't you ever read the medical journals?"

I do not, in fact. Neither did he when we were on the high school swim team together.

He went on, "They'll put your Mom's organs to good use, don't worry. It was a commendable gesture on her part...something you should think about doing yourself."

"Uh, Mike...can they keep a brain alive...without the body?"

"Is that what they're working on now?" He chuckled. "If anyone can, they can at the Institute. Thanks for letting me in on it..."

"But it *can* be done?"

"Well, I can't tell you how to do it...not yet. But if scientists can clone a complex organism from a few cells, keeping a brain alive ought to be nothing more than a matter of...plumbing, one day."

"Thanks, Mike..." I hung up. I couldn't help thinking about how costly plumbers can be.

The next call I made was to my lawyer. I knew this would be more difficult. Baxter – of Boggs, Briggs, and Baxter – assumed I was calling him again because I was anxious about pushing Mom's will through probate as quickly as possible.

He was working on it, he said curtly.

"No...I've...uh, got a different question..."

"Time is money. Spit it out..."

"What if somebody they think is dead...comes back?"

"Like a missing person who returns?

"No...what if the doctors say someone's died – written a death certificate and all, even buried the body – and then they discover how to bring them back to life?"

"This is pretty hypothetical...why do you want to know?"

"I was just...talking...with one of the guys..."

"I usually get a hundred bucks an hour...for talking."

"I'll send you a check." (Goddamn lawyers!) "What are the legal rights of the...*formerly* deceased?"

"You mean like if one of those screwballs in California who had themselves flash frozen after dying ever gets revived?"

MOM

"Yeah. If they can bring them back to life, what does that mean...for the heirs? Do they have to return everything to the person who...died?"

"If the will hasn't gone through yet, probably yes. If it has, and the inheritors are in possession of the property of a person who really was dead...that's a good question. The courts have never ruled. It's never happened..."

"Thanks." I let the sarcasm drip, "That helps me a lot..."

"You'll be getting my bill."

The last phone call was to Lorna, girlfriend of the moment. I had to wait while the foreman got her off the line. For my purposes, Lorna – well-endowed, not too smart, and more than willing – was perfect, if not challenging. Clever women never appealed much to me, and serious "relationships" were strenuously to be avoided. Lorna and I had a date for that night, and I'd had plans to end up in a blessedly empty house. I knew I should cancel the evening.

"Lorna...baby...how ya doin'?"

With a mouth full of chewing gum, she murmured something indistinct but sweet, I'm sure. While Mom was chair-ridden, except for the last few weeks, Lorna and I had been able to come back after a date, exchange pleasantries, and then slip away to my room. Although the house is small, with paper thin walls, Mom either slept snoring in the chair or had the television on LOUD. Lorna still lives with her parents and comes from a big, noisy family, so she doesn't need a lot of privacy. But now I didn't know, at least not tonight.

"Lorna...honey...I've got to break our date..."

She took it well. Needed no explanation. Said she would go bowling with the girls. I hoped so; Lorna is the kind who shouldn't be left too long with her motor running.

"Thanks, doll," I told her, "I'll make it up to you. I promise..."

I didn't stay in the workshop even though I was really enthusiastic about something I'd been working on, something that could make me a million: a fully portable bidet, one that hooks up to any commode. Everyone knows how popular bidets are. Why not a set-up that can be attached, quickly and easily, to an ordinary toilet? With my prototype, you just place the water jet under the seat, connect a hose to a faucet (usually the sink or bathtub) and adjust the taps for temperature. Then have yourself a blast! There were a few bugs in the system still, and Lorna was helping me work them out. I

MOM

figured if I got it so even she could use it, my bidet would be foolproof. But how could I stay in the workshop thinking about feminine hygiene while Mom was home in the front room in a state of suspended animation? Besides, there was nothing else to hold me in the city, which in March had all the charm of Zagreb. At least I'd beat the traffic for once.

When I arrived home the house was a hive of activity. I noticed a new power line, a thick one, had been run from the utility pole on the street. To elude Hugo, I went in the cellar door and sneaked down the back stairs. I wanted to see for myself what'd happened since I left. I found the basement filled floor to ceiling with racks of equipment packed so tight a person could scarcely slide between the rows. Everywhere pilot lights blinked, gauges danced, and electric motors hummed as multicolored liquids bubbled through transparent tubes. A big computer dominated one wall, apparently controlling it all. Though the furnace had been turned off, it felt warm down there from so much electronic stuff. In fact, I even spied a couple of the "alien invaders" (technicians) installing an air conditioning unit in a below ground window.

I ran up the inside stairs two at a time. I had to speak to Hugo. Standing in the front room, he was wreathed in smiles of self-satisfaction.

"Everything is per-*fekt*," he proclaimed Teutonically. "We were just waiting for you."

We? Apart from me, he was the only person in the room. Then I remembered Mom. I said:

"Before you…uh, turn Mom on, I've got to ask something…"

"Yes…"

"Before, was she truly…dead?" The question was bothering me for more than legal reasons. "Dead as a doornail dead?" I needed to know.

"Of course…legally and clinically dead," Hugo explained. "Our experiment would not have been ethical otherwise. We could not have saved her, if that is what you are worried about. We could not have done anything more to prolong her life or we would have. The body – the life – failed totally. *Kaput*…though briefly. Only then did we restore functioning, in the laboratory…to the current, comatose state you see here."

He looked lovingly at the head.

"So…we can proceed?" he said. I saw he could hardly wait.

"Sure…"

MOM

Still, for some reason, I wanted to buy time.

"But...explain to me first how all this works." With a wave of the hand I indicated the whole setup. "I have a professional interest. I'm an inventor..."

Hugo was delighted. Despite his eagerness to continue, he loved lecturing about engineering as much as a Mercedes-Benz salesman.

"Life support is provided by the equipment in the basement," he began. "We have dispensed with the messy machinery of the body."

I *like* the messy machinery of the body.

"The head, however, retains its physical capabilities. Stephanie, Mrs. Kravath, will be able to function entirely as before...from the chin up. She has all the senses — sight, smell, taste, touch, and hearing — along with normal reflexes. What is more, she has active control of the muscles of her face, jaw, and part of the throat. Better than some quadriplegics..." he enthused, really getting into it. "Without saying, it goes that she maintains all her mental faculties."

I didn't want Great Moments in Medicine. I needed practical information.

"How does she eat?" I innocently inquired. Mom loved to eat.

Hugo was shocked that I'd asked. He said, "Why, she is fed intravenously, of course. Organic processes are taken care of externally...biomechanically. Even respiration. She should receive nothing by mouth. *Noth-ing!*" (I couldn't help thinking of Schultz on *"Hogan's Heroes."*) "Except for a little moisture from time to time..."

Besides, I wondered, where would it go?

He went on: "Your mother will be able to communicate quite normally. Although there is no larynx, we have implanted an artificial voice box like the ones used by people who have had their vocal cords removed. And we engineered an air flow since there is no breath...no lungs, as you would know them."

All right, all right. I've seen the gadgets laryngectomies use. They hold a little electric vibrator over an opening at the base of their throat. Those things have to be switched on manually, though. I asked:

"How does she turn on the...uh, speaking equipment?"

"Unconsciously...for all practical purposes." Hugo was really proud of this. "Sensors pick up minute contractions of throat muscles used naturally in speaking and automatically activate the system...before the words are out of her mouth, one might say." He started to speak faster himself. "Eventually she will be interactive...with the telephone, computers, TV, stereo, the DVD player..."

DVD? Computers? Mom never could manage all that herself before. It sounded as if she was going to become a regular home entertainment center.

"Maybe you better tell me what she *can't* do...besides dance."

"Well, she cannot turn her head or raise or lower it without external mechanical assistance. No spinal cord, you see. But we will teach her how to use eye movements to activate servos installed in the life support module she rests upon – the black box – which will allow her to swivel and rotate. It *is* a little tricky..."

For the first time, he sounded unsure of himself.

"It will be...a learning experience for all involved," he decided, happy again.

"I'll bet!" I tried to imagine Mom swiveling and rotating.

"*Also...*" *sprach* Hugo, "Shall we commence?"

"Go ahead..." I said. His excitement was becoming contagious. "Give 'er the juice."

He mumbled into a walkie-talkie and bent low over Mom. The lights in the room dimmed, like during an electrocution in a grade-B prison movie. It was very dramatic, but I couldn't see that anything was happening at first. I wondered when I'd notice a change. All at once, I came up with a dozen questions I hadn't thought to ask. There was a lot I ought to know. I should've found out whether Mom would revive slowly or come back instantaneously, whether she'd understand what was going on or remember what happened before. Would she lose some memory – like a computer hard drive that's been worked on? (Hard drive...that about described Mom's brain.) Had *she* been properly prepared for the experience?

How was she going to feel? Would she be happy? Scared? Disoriented? Tired? Mom had been pretty fussy, demanding even, about her creature comforts. Would she be comfortable now? What'll she ask for first? And what if she wants something we can't give her? What if she's senile? Amnesiac? Crazy? How long will it take for her to begin to talk again? I couldn't imagine what the first words out of the mouth

MOM

of someone who'd just returned from the dead would be. Maybe we should write them down, or tape them. And—

Mom's eyes flew open so suddenly I jumped back. Then I rushed to her side, crouching down so I could be eye to eye with her.

"Mom! Mom!" I couldn't help shouting though I was inches from her face. "Do you know me? I'm you son! You're back! You're home? Do you understand?" I was yelling as if trying to communicate across a great void.

"Mom!"

There was a very audible click and the whirr of an electric motor. The whole head tipped back slightly as the lower jaw opened. Mom's lips moved stiffly and words followed as if out of sync. In a voice that sounded like E.T., the Extraterrestrial, she said:

"I didn't think I'd died and gone to heaven..."

Good old Mom...as sarcastic as always.

Another click, the whirring stopped, then silence.

Hugo explained the click and whirr: "That is the speech unit fan motor...turning on and off..."

"Mom…" I was almost moved to tears. "Is there anything you want? Anything I can do for you?"

Her eyes darted eerily around the room.

Click.

Whirr.

Then the flat, vibrato voice again:

"Get the hell out of the way and turn on the TV…I want to watch my shows."

Click. Whirr.

That was all. Over and out.

"She is tired…" Hugo suggested.

And cranky, I thought. So what else is new?

"Let me make some tests…" Hugo was asking either Mom or me; I wasn't sure who.

Dutifully, I turned on the TV. Already I was looking forward to getting out of the loop once Mom became "interactive." While Hugo worked she watched *"Wheel of Fortune"* with such consuming interest that I could go into the kitchen unnoticed. With time to think about it, I decided Mom was no more (or less) disturbing to look at like this than somebody in an iron lung. After half an hour, Hugo came searching for me.

"Everything has gone precisely as planned," he announced with pride.

MOM

"Well...then, tell me," I asked, "who's going to pay to keep her alive and kicking from now on?" I'd spoken before I thought how, given Mom's bodiless condition, the expression didn't fit.

"Not to worry. This is an experiment. The Institute will assume all expenses...in perpetuity. But your mother will need a care-giver," Hugo said very seriously, "You."

I didn't like the sound of "in perpetuity." Or even less of "...you" (meaning me).

"We have arranged for a Visiting Nurse to come as well..."

I could only picture some old battleaxe who'd known Florence Nightingale when she was still called "Flo." It was too easy to imagine Mom and her conspiring, ganging up, against me. It'd happened all the time with Mom and her sisters.

"But how can I maintain the support equipment?" I whined. "I'm an inventor, not a scientist. I'm good with my hands...a mechanic, an engineer even, but..."

"It is all automated," Hugo said with that "tut, tut" tone to his voice again. "The crew and I will check in at frequent intervals. And there are alarms. When you are in hospital, in an intensive care unit on life support machines...do you think someone is monitoring them all the time?"

That was a chilling thought.

"O.K...but now that Mom's back," I struggled with what I was trying to say, "we don't want to lose her again..." (*Do we?* I was beginning to wonder).

"I told you, be happy...do not worry. There are back-ups built into the system. If electricity fails, batteries in the basement can maintain operation for a full twenty-four hours. And a generator will kick in afterwards to recharge them indefinitely."

Like a hybrid car, I thought, then asked, "What if there's a fire or something? She would be trapped..."

"*Nein, nein.* She can be moved without advance preparation. The support module is portable; once charged, it can be disconnected from the host system and keep functioning independently for four hours. In fact, you may want to take Stephanie outside for a little airing...or a ride in the car when the weather gets better."

"That black box can do the work of all the stuff in the basement?" I was astounded. "It's so small..." About the size of a big man's torso, I figured.

MOM

"The magic of miniaturization. At about twelve percent of total body weight, it takes a lot less to keep a head alive than an entire human being. But only for four hours…"

"What happens if the time limit is exceeded?"

"A 'life preserver' system automatically engages to return the subject safely and painlessly to a comatose state. Essentially, that is how your mother arrived here. Then the subject can be revived simply by reconnecting to the main equipment."

I noticed Hugo seemed more confident talking about a "subject" than a real person.

"Inducing such a 'sleep' may even be useful intentionally for dull road trips," he said, "like motoring across southern Illinois…"

I wasn't comfortable with it.

"How long can she last…in a comatose state?"

"With no deterioration at all? About thirty days under normal conditions of standard temperature and pressure, average humidity, etc. Longer, if kept cool and dry."

Like a cured ham, I thought.

"When she's hooked up is there anything that's likely to hurt her?"

"Apart from gross physical trauma, probably no. She is very resilient. After all, bodies usually fail before brains."

"So...ah...how long can she be expected to uh, *live*...like this?"

"We do not really know, but it stands to reason a person will last a very long time if their organs (or substitutes) can be repaired or replaced indefinitely. And Stephanie's can...now that hers are in the basement, so to speak." Hugo beamed. "She could last longer than you or I."

"Oh, great..." I thought of asking for more info about the effects of "gross physical trauma," but decided not to risk possibly tipping my hand.

Hugo looked at his watch. He had to be off, he said, it was a long drive to the Institute.

"You're going to leave someone here to look after things, aren't you?" I asked desperately, "the first night and all..."

"Not to worry. You can handle it. Everything is up and running and the equipment does not require constant attention. Tonight, all your mother may want is rest, although she actually will sleep very little...the brain requires less recovery time than other organs. Just let her stay there and get acclimated."

MOM

Let her stay? I thought, where's she going to go? Still, I protested:

"But I don't know anything yet...about how to take care of her like this..."

"What is to know? You took care of her, all of her, for eighteen months. It should be a lot easier now. Remember, no messy machinery of the body..."

"What if there's an emergency?" I sputtered.

"The worst that will happen is she slips back into unconsciousness...like sleep. Then call us at the Institute. What can go wrong? Any problem can be corrected."

Unconsciousness...sleep. It seemed more like *death* to me.

"Besides," Hugo persisted, "it is only for a matter of hours. I have asked the nurse to make her first call bright and early tomorrow morning. She has been trained by us. She will begin to train *you* tomorrow...and start getting Stephanie (he looked at Mom lovingly) fully operational, too."

I wondered how long he and Mom had been on a first name basis.

"See..." he said, "the nurse lives right in town. She is on call. I will give you a phone number. She can be here in five minutes..."

I figured it'd be all right then. Maybe.

"*Ja-a...*" Hugo cajoled (as if talking to a little *Enkel*-biter). "Do not worry...be happy."

Jawohl!

Hugo bade Mom a misty good-bye, promised he'd be back soon, and then he and his minions marched out. It looked like quitting time on a sci-fi movie set.

I was home alone with Mom. Again.

Click. Whirr.

"Change the channel...change the channel..." was all Mom had to say to me.

While she was sick, especially the last few months, Mom had been glued to the TV. It was because the TV was such a good companion that I'd gone out and gotten an expensive big screen model for her – high def, the best. I didn't have to babysit so much with a hundred and eighty-some cable channels for her to choose from, day and night. I guess she got used to it. But at that time she'd at least been able to work the remote control for herself, right up to the end almost. Now, until they made her "interactive," she was helpless.

Except for me.

I hunted around the channels for an old movie. Mom always loved old movies.

"There...stop!" she commanded. "That one..."

MOM

Not even a "thank you."

I sat down in Mom's old chair to try and watch with her. The show had already started and I wasn't even sure which movie it was. I got a pain in the neck from the way I had to turn to see the TV (Mom could see great). I couldn't concentrate, anyway; I had too much on my mind, too many questions. But Mom looked completely absorbed. Her eyes danced along with the characters on the screen — Gene Kelley and Leslie Caron, I think. At one time, Mom had been quite a dancer herself. I wondered how she felt now, like this. I thought I should say something.

"You okay?" I asked.

She didn't reply.

"Is there anything I can do for you? Anything at all?"

Click. Whirr.

"Turn up the volume…"

Click. Whirr.

I did. And I let her watch for a while. But finally, I had to ask:

"Mom…what was it like? Can you tell me?"

She didn't answer. Her eyes didn't even flick my way. Yet I was sure she knew what I meant. I tried again:

"What was it like…*to be dead?*"

She simply clicked on – "I don't want to talk about it" – and off.

Conversation over.

I got up and went into the kitchen. She must've experienced something…something extraordinary. But she wouldn't tell me about it. It was especially mean of her because Mom knew I was interested in that sort of thing. I'd gotten my interest from her, actually. Before, she'd been into "other worldly" pursuits – Eastern philosophy, ESP, the occult. I used to laugh and call her "Madame Blavatsky." Now she had firsthand knowledge of the Other Side and wouldn't share it with me. I felt hurt, and angry. I thought she was being very petty.

Then—

Click. Whirr.

"Bring me my glasses. My eyes are getting tired without 'em…"

"I thought they buried them with you…in that little blue clutch you always carried." I tried to sound comically ghoulish "…*even beyond the grave.*"

"Very funny…the other pair, in my nightstand drawer…"

In the nightstand? I couldn't remember; how could she? Yet there they were, just where she said they'd be. I wondered if maybe time

MOM

had stood still for her. She certainly acted as if it had; she never missed a beat. I stood in front of her, snapped open the frames, and pushed the glasses onto her face and over her ears. I guess I wasn't very gentle. I wasn't used to putting glasses on somebody else's head.

Click. Whirr.

"I'm not a department store dummy! Take it easy..."

"Sorry..."

I backed away, drinking in the scene of Mom with the lights turned down, home again in the warm glow of the TV, looking like the Wizard of Oz in bifocals. I shook my head and went into the kitchen to get myself something to eat.

Click. Whirr.

"I'm thirsty..."

I knew what to do. I wet a clean cloth with cool water, wrung it out, and stuck it in Mom's mouth so she could suck on it. She didn't much like that, but I could tell she understood it was all she was allowed. Not too difficult. I started feeling more confident. I took a moment to study her and noticed she had her dentures in. I wondered whether she'd gone through the whole ordeal with her teeth. Mom was pretty vain, so I wouldn't have been surprised, but I knew better than to ask. I did ask:

"You want me to take your teeth out for the night?"

"Leave my teeth alone…I look funny enough already."

"Who's to see? Besides, what do you need teeth for?"

Maybe that was a little insensitive.

"You wouldn't understand. Go away…"

All right. It was getting late, so I went to my room down the hall (there is no upstairs) and lay on the bed with my shoes off but clothes on.

Click. Whirr. Click. Whirr.

Like a dripping faucet, I couldn't *not* listen for it.

Click. Whirr.

I got up and padded the few feet back to the front room.

"What?" I asked.

"I didn't say anything…"

Click. Whirr.

I returned to my room. Even with the door closed, even with the TV blasting, I could hear it: Click. Whirr. By accident or design, Mom was turning the speaking thing on and off, on and off, over and over. Maybe it gave her a little tickle; God knows she didn't have many thrills now. It didn't do anything for my

MOM

relaxation, though. I had an idea and went back to the front room.

"Maybe you ought to get some sleep..." I said as I picked the glass globe off the floor where Hugo had left it.

Click. Whirr.

"I've already had the sleep of the dead."

"Well, some rest then..."

I tried to position the globe over Mom's head.

"What do you think I am," she buzzed angrily, "a goddamn goldfish?" She stared in horror at the globe. "I'm never going in that thing again. Never! All white and frosty, that thing is...*nothingness!*"

"Bad idea..." I admitted, and put it where she couldn't see it. Maybe that was what death was like?

Sleep apparently was unnecessary for Mom, and nearly impossible for me now. I found myself waiting for the "click, whirr" the way a new mother listens for a change in her baby's breathing. I was going to need a long time to get used to this. And Mom didn't have any consideration for how late it was when she did summon me, intentionally, to change channels after a couple of hours or so. I tried to find another movie she'd want to watch – a long one, just starting – so I could get some rest.

I'd half dropped off to sleep before I was jolted by a wail that had to be the closest thing to a scream Mom's speaking equipment could produce. Still sleepy, I stumbled, bleary-eyed and shoeless, from my bed to the front room. There I woke up – fast.

"Mom!"

Her head was whipping from side to side and up and down – rolling, zooming, sometimes making figure-eights – going faster and faster all the time. It was turning so far I couldn't help wondering if it was going to spin completely around, like in *"The Exorcist."* I hadn't thought she was able to move her head at all yet. Then I realized it wasn't Mom's doing. Her eyes, like ping-pong balls being volleyed back and forth, bounced in a direction opposite to the out-of-control head movement. Terrified and dizzy, she looked bilious.

"What's happening!" I yelled.

Speechless, she just clicked and whirred.

I didn't know how to stop her. I ran up and tried the first thing I could think of: I grabbed Mom's moving head under one arm in a headlock. With my other hand, I held onto her forehead, accidently knocking her glasses off.

MOM

The force turning Mom's head was tremendous. She got her voice back right away:

"You're hurting me! You idiot...you're hurting me! Ow. *Ow-w...*"

I let her go. Why'd she have to get so huffy? I thought at least I'd slowed her. Then I remembered something Hugo told me about the head-turning apparatus, how it worked from eye movements.

"Mom! *Mom!*" I yelled, crouching beside her, pointing to the TV. "Look at the TV. Don't take your eyes off it..." A flag was fluttering for the station's signoff. "Don't take your eyes off that flag..."

She zeroed in on the screen and her movement gradually slowed. She didn't quite trust me though, and glanced away out of the corner of an eye. Her head started to barrel roll again.

"No! No! Look at the TV. Only the TV..."

Mom stared at the grand old flag as steadily as a veteran on the Fourth of July.

"Your eye movements..." I paused to catch my breath. "Your eye movements activate the turntable...somehow. Guess the Institute hasn't gotten all the bugs out yet."

"Those morons..." she growled through gritted teeth, looking straight ahead. Then she softened and, I thought, almost smiled. "Hugo will fix it...he can fix anything." Now Mom was afraid to look anywhere but at the TV, which had started broadcasting a test pattern.

"No..." I began to laugh, "You don't have to stare that way all the time. Only looking out the corners of your eyes – or 'way up or down – engages the servo system...I think."

"I felt so helpless..." she said, wincing as I replaced her glasses – carefully, this time.

"I know..."

Mom said, "I need something. I need...a drink."

"I'll wet the wash cloth again..."

"No...I mean a *real* drink."

This wasn't the time to argue with her. I got some slivovitz out of the cabinet and soaked the cloth in it. What could be the harm? I poured a stiff one for myself, too, changed the TV channel, and found a movie with Fred Astaire and Ginger Rogers, *"Flying Down to Rio."* I shoved Mom's old chair around beside her so I could see better and sat back to watch. I figured I wouldn't be able to sleep myself after all the excitement.

Click. Whirr.

MOM

"Gimme another shot of that joy juice, son..."

I took some more, too. Then—

"Son..."

"What?"

"Thanks..."

Click. Whirr.

I fell asleep almost immediately.

II

I WOKE TO THE SOUND OF SOMEONE pounding on the door. Whoever it was must've tried the bell first, but after listening to the "click, whirr" so many times I'd tuned out all electronic noises.

"Coming!" I bellowed.

The girl standing out in the morning sunshine looked to be about twenty-six or seven. And was she nice! Small without being delicate, neat without being prim, straightforward but stylish in a blue cloth coat. What struck me most was her strawberry blonde hair. From photos, I knew it was like Mom's hair when she was that age. At first I couldn't think who it might be at nine a.m. on a Saturday. Then I saw she had a uniform on under the coat and a good-sized case by her side.

"Of course!" I cried. "The visiting nurse...*angel of mercy*..."

I rushed to open the door, not thinking how I must've looked like hell, unshaved and as rumpled as the bed I had not, in fact, slept in.

"C'mon in..." I grabbed for her case. "Here...let me help you with that..."

She stood her ground.

"I'm May…May Desjardins – from the Visiting Nurse Association…"

"It's okay…you don't have to show your credentials or anything like that…we've been expecting you."

Then I realized she was insisting on a modicum of decorum. *Introduce, yourself, dummy…*

"Uh…I'm Steve Kravath…"

She offered her hand. I clasped it, maybe too warmly. May had a no-nonsense handshake. I went for the case again.

"I can manage, thanks," said she.

Strike One?

She hefted the bag herself, having more difficulty getting it over the threshold than she let on, and lugged it into the front room. As she approached Mom, I was left with the Saturday morning cartoons on the TV.

"Mrs. Kravath? Stephanie Kravath?"

"Yes, dear. Oh, yes…"

"I'm May, from the VNA. Sent by the Institute. I'll usually be stopping by Monday through Friday."

May…from the VNA. I liked the sound of that.

I should've made introductions.

MOM

"I've got something for you..." May said to Mom, delving into her bag to bring out, of all things – a wig. Though this must've been arranged before her death, Mom seemed as surprised as I was. Her eyes got so wide I worried her head might start to spin again. The wig was exactly the tint of Mom's hair maybe fifty years ago. No matter that she hadn't looked anything like that for decades, she thought it was great.

May was *in*.

"I matched it to the color of my own hair," she explained. "I know it's not perfect, but it's close to yours...isn't it?"

"It's lovely, dear...lovely. You're so kind. Thank you..."

For some reason, I could swear Mom winked at me.

May fluffed and combed the hairpiece – a short, pert, fly-away cut that fit Mom's feisty personality – holding it so Mom could see, and they clucked over it for a while. Then May stretched the thing onto Mom's bald pate. And she was transformed! Mom had no eyebrows or eyelashes, no body hair at all (*heh*...no body). Still, she was a woman again. She almost looked grandmotherly, except there wasn't a wisp of grey in her coif, which reminded me of the color of pink champagne. May produced a good-sized hanging mirror from her case and held it so Mom could admire herself. For the first time since she returned, Mom really smiled. For some reason, I didn't think she was able to, I guess because Hugo hadn't mentioned anything about it. May held up the heavy mirror until I saw that her arms — fine boned, with a hint of the freckles all carrot tops seem to have — were starting to tremble. I offered to take over (and finally scored some points, I hoped).

Next, on the "shoulders" of Mom's black box, May arranged what looked like a whole cosmetics counter, lights and all, and proceeded to make Mom up. She penciled in eyebrows that to me could've passed for real. She used liner and mascara to define Mom's washed-out peepers and carefully applied eye shadow to give more color and depth. Despite Mom's constant blinking, May managed to fasten on fluttering false lashes. Then she added a touch of blush to Mom's cheeks — up high, by the cheekbones — that brought a glow to the otherwise bloodless-looking alabaster skin. A little *cerise* lipstick restored a vivaciousness I hadn't seen since before Mom got sick. I thought it was a bit much, though, to doll up a talking head. So I had to be smart:

MOM

"Nurse 'Mary Kay,' eh..."

The two of them shot looks like daggers my way.

"He doesn't understand," Mom clacked, her dentures loosening, "how a woman feels."

Strike Two. But I knew how to redeem myself. I went into Mom's old bedroom and rummaged through the dresser until I found a pair of fake sapphire and diamond earrings she'd always liked. I came back and dangled them in front of her. She tried to be nonchalant, but I could tell she was eager to accept the peace offering. Mom always would fall for anything that made her look more "beautiful." As May put the earrings on her, I hung the mirror on the back of a chair and positioned it so Mom could look at herself to her heart's content.

"Why don't you and May go have a cup of coffee in the kitchen?" she said. "I'll be all right alone for a few minutes."

Mom had been a big coffee drinker. Maybe she was sensitive now about people enjoying something in front of her that she couldn't manage herself. Besides, I figured she wanted to study her makeover at leisure. Maybe I'd get another chance with May, too. Sitting at the kitchen table while Mr. Coffee was doing his thing, I tried to impress her.

"I'm…uh, an inventor, you know…"

"Oh? What kinds of things do you invent?"

"Uh…things that make everyday life a little…easier. Maybe a little more fun…"

"You make a living doing that?"

"Sure…a *good* living," I lied. "The products are developed by a number of companies and marketed through mail order catalogues." I didn't mention they're mostly in the novelty line.

"Like…for instance?" she asked. At least she was interested.

I knew better than to begin with the bidet, not with this gal. Should I tell her about my *Get It Hot at Home* pizza warmer?" Naw…it'd been obsoleted already, bested by improved delivery technology. (I always was "inventing" things that had already been invented, it seemed.) How about the *AllDay Diapers* with silica gel inserts? Or the *KeepRollin'* spinoff, redesigned for long-haul truckers? No… not enough of a success, commercially.

"Well…my *InstaKool* drink cooler, for example," I finally decided. "I got the idea from the guys down at the firehouse. When they're dying for a cold one and all the beer is warm, they set off a CO_2 fire extinguisher right on top of a six-pack. Without knowing it, they're using a fundamental principle of physics. Y'see, when

MOM

a gas expands very rapidly after being under pressure it becomes super cold, practically like dry ice. It'd freeze off your...well, you get the idea. I just miniaturized the whole thing, designed a sleeve with a little CO_2 cartridge the size they use in soda siphons. The *InstaKool* looks like a World War II Kraut "potato masher" grenade – guys like that. Slip a couple cans of beer...or soda in the sleeve, pull the pin, and *whoosh!* a frosty one for you and a friend..."

May sat there, tapping her foot. (Should I have mentioned that I've got an engineering degree?) I thought maybe she had limited interest in technical matters. So much the better; I never did fancy smart women. I figured it was time to hand her a line, so I tried the oldest one in the book:

"You new in town?" When I met her at the door I'd noticed her car had out-of-state plates.

A slow "Ye-ess..." made me think I might be getting somewhere. Hurrying heedlessly down the path to self-destruction, I continued:

"If we can sneak out after Mom's had her oil changed and fluids topped off, maybe I can show you around..."

I didn't realize the sparkle in May's green eyes (Mom's were a little more blue) was the flash of quiet anger. Then it came out—

"Don't you understand...the *psychological* well-being of a patient is every bit as important as the physical?"

She was mad. *Stee-rike three!*

"You're going to have to learn a few things," she scolded me, "about *sensitivity,* so you can take care of your mother...*in every way.*"

I don't know why that got me so riled. Maybe I could see I'd crashed and burned and wasn't going to get to first base.

"You look..." I cut in. "I took care of Mom, *all of her,* not just the...the *bodiless horsewoman* here, for a year and a half – when she was sick, when she was dying, when she wasn't the way she is now...tough as a tank turret! Don't *you* try to tell *me* how to take care of her. Hugo can give me all the techno crap I need. The rest I know already. Believe me, *I know!*" The force of my anger surprised me. "I stayed with Mom, stayed up with her nights, gave her medicines, then painkillers...around the clock. I fed her, washed her, *even wiped her ass!*"

May didn't say anything. But she didn't flinch, either.

"Then...it was over – the end that comes so everybody else can go on living...in peace. Isn't that why they say, "Rest in Peace?" And what happens? She's back, perched on that box…forever, maybe. She'll be demanding, domineering, taking over again, as soon as she's able."

I must've been shouting. Mom had to yell to make herself heard.

"Hey…" she piped up. "HEY!"

I still didn't understand how she was able to raise the volume of her voice at will like that. There was a lot Hugo hadn't told me. May and I trooped into the front room.

"I want my sisters to visit. Give 'em a call, will you, son? Tell them to come by tomorrow. Tomorrow's Sunday, isn't it? They'll be able to make it on Sunday afternoon."

I wondered how I should explain Mom's new *persona* to them. Oh, hell, I thought, they probably already knew more about it than I did.

"May, dear…" Mom began to wheedle, "you can stop by tomorrow, too, can't you…just to touch me up a little? So my sisters can see. I know Sunday's not a scheduled day for you, but just this once…"

"Actually, Mrs. Kravath, I'm going out of town tonight…to visit a girlfriend. Won't be back 'til late Sunday evening, I'm afraid."

"See, Mom," I said, "she has a *life*…"

"That's all right then, dear." Mom considered her makeup in the mirror again. "It'll last, won't it?"

"Well...the makeup and wig really ought to come off at night. Your skin should be cleansed, to let the pores breathe, than massaged with a moisturizer...to keep it supple." May glanced wickedly my way. "Your son's going to have to do all that for you now..."

"But just this once, can't we..."

May interrupted, "I can show Steve how to make you up."

Click. Whirr.

"Oh, no! He's too rough. He'll poke an eye out. Make me look like a clown..."

May shook her head.

"I'll only be able to do it for you on the days when I'm here..."

I was glad to see she was being firm with Mom; *somebody* had to be.

"If you want to look nice on weekends, too, you'll have to trust your son."

I wasn't happy with that. I agreed with Mom; I'm no cosmetologist.

"He doesn't know anything..."

"As I said, I'll teach him. He can practice on me first."

MOM

What followed was one of the most strangely sensual hours I've ever spent. May set a collection of pots, paints, and powders on a table, draped a towel around her shoulders, and placed a straight-backed chair where the daylight from the big picture window could play fully on her face. She sat down calmly with her hands in her lap and told me to use cold cream to remove her "base."

"Base?" I asked.

May had almost no makeup on; didn't need any. The subtle sheen of the powder she wore came off easily with the cream. I stroked her a little longer than necessary. It was a real pleasure for me, and she didn't seem to mind. With her face wiped clean and looking as fresh as the new morning streaming in, I thought how May's beauty showed best when she was *au naturel*. She then instructed me in the daily ritual every woman knows. Making May up, I felt like an actor's "dresser" – an apprentice dresser, to be sure. I wondered whether it was harder to do this for someone else or for yourself. I made lots of mistakes and almost did get a brush in her eye once. But May was patient, even laughed from time to time. She had a beautiful laugh, spilling freely like falling water. I was glad to uncover a good-natured side to her. I also thought she was clever to have me use colors and textures appropriate for Mom, an older woman. Yet even the wrong makeup, and my occasional ham-handedness, couldn't diminish the good looks that were May's birthright.

After my outburst in the kitchen a while ago, I did all I could to "play nice" now. I paid attention to everything May told me and tried hard to do my best. No kidding around. If I didn't understand something, I asked for clarification and respected her expertise. I wanted May to see me as more than a male chauvinist. And I liked being able to look at her without the appearance of staring. Still, I wondered if I'd ever be able to make up for my bad start.

It took some time but, by trying over and over, I think I got fairly good at making her up. May praised my perseverance. Even Mom whirred her grudging approval. *Amazing!* One more wipe-down and May used the mirror to restore her own face much more swiftly and surely than I could have. Doing it right there in front of me like that seemed an intimate act. Or maybe an act of indifference, of total disregard for my presence. Was I just "one of the girls" now? I hoped not.

MOM

I felt as if something had been left unfinished when May closed her case to get ready to go. She kissed Mom lightly on one powdered cheek and left the mirror, and a collection of hypoallergenic cosmetics, behind.

"See you Monday…" she told Mom.

"See you…" I said hopefully, trying to sound cheery as May stood at the door. "I guess I *do* have a few things to learn…"

She smiled (in triumph or understanding?) and started off toward her little compact car parked at the curb. She trundled the cosmetics case by herself into the back of the car and drove away. I couldn't help watching after her a long time.

Mom broke my reverie.

Click. Whirr.

"Get on the phone…"

"Yes, Mom…" I sighed.

It took most of the afternoon to reach Mom's four sisters – the whole tribe – who, as always on a Saturday, were out and about. Good thing it wasn't yard sale season. I was ticked to find how much better informed they were than I'd been about Mom's dealings with the Eterna Institute. Mom tells them a lot more than she tells me, probably because she doesn't think I'm grown up enough yet to confide in.

Mom's sisters were awaiting the announcement of her homecoming the way normal people anticipate joyful greetings on the birth of an expected baby. At least it made my job easier.

Yes, each and every one of them could be here tomorrow afternoon. I didn't have to worry about a thing, they said. They would bring food.

Sunday, around noon, I slapped a fresh coat of paint on Mom and stood by as the one p.m. rendezvous time approached. The aunts trooped in, kissed her ("How *well* you look, dear") and immediately set up a *Kaffeeklatsch* in the front room, scarfing each other's baked goodies by the plateful. Just like always. Mom had loved the "fat pills" of Mitteleuropa, too; now she eyed them as lustfully as a high school boy let loose in the girls' locker room. I alone seemed to notice Mom's discomfort at nourishment being so near and yet so far away. Only Mom's family could flock around a dear departed talking head, stuffing themselves and acting as if there was nothing extremely bizarre about it.

Speaking of bizarre, sometimes I almost forget I grew up the lone male in this tribe of overbearing women, with no father or uncles to turn to. Mom was the only one of the five

MOM

sisters to marry (don't ask me why) and, perhaps because he lacked the constitution to survive in so hostile an environment, Dad didn't last long at all. His side of the family lived far away; Mom's did not – unfortunately. I was lucky Mom had the sense to keep me from being raised as a Little Lord Fauntleroy, or worse, which is what her sisters would have done to me if they'd been given half a chance, I'm sure. I hate to think what I would've become then. Instead, I had a pretty happy childhood.

By the age of ten or eleven, however, my ability to do things the ladies couldn't do for themselves piqued their interest in me again. These things included a wide range of tasks that involved first elbow grease, then physical strength, and later, mechanical or technical skills – all coupled with a willingness to get dirty – attributes my aunts lacked in spades. It proved a liability because "little Stevie" soon was in constant demand. My life became kind of like being a harem slave in reverse, with just one of me to service a whole passel of demanding lady pashas who had no end of projects they needed me to put my hand to. Not that I ever got much credit for it. I was supposed to *want* to bust my butt for the ladies all the time "...*so's to prove I'm A Man,*" like in an old western movie.

There was a silver lining to the dark DIY cloud hanging over me in that I got to be really handy. My aunts prophesied I'd "…make someone a great husband someday," although I wondered how *they* could know, given their lack of personal experience. It sounded too much like a life sentence to me. Still, I segued from being a fixer-upper to my true calling as an engineer and inventor, so I guess the training wasn't all bad. And I learned patience, too, having to negotiate all the time with the gaggle of silly geese who make up my family. I guess this stood me in good stead for enduring Mom's debut as a semi-automaton.

I was surprised when Hugo turned up in his best brown suit later in the afternoon. "I could not keep away from *my girl,*" he explained. He even brought flowers. To my family, flowers at any time other than birthdays, funerals, and registered anniversaries are a token of true love. Mom glowed. Hugo sounded like Henry Kissinger as he talked to the old dames. They were impressed with his accent and thought him "cultured." He loaded them with the same information about how Mom's plumbing works that he'd provided me on Friday. I don't know how much they understood. This time Hugo stressed how easy it was going to be (for me) to

MOM

take care of Mom. "A piece of cake..." he said. Now, *cake* they could understand. No reason then for a put-upon, care-giving son to complain. "Do not worry...be happy."

The sisters tittered compliments to Mom about Hugo. What did they see in him? They talked as if he and Mom were an item. Maybe because he was the only male who doted on her now? And dote he did. He couldn't have found Mom more entrancing if she came with all her original equipment; in fact, for him, her disembodied state was the attraction, I'm sure. As for Mom, she ate it up. Unfortunately, that was the only thing she *was* able to eat. While the sisters stuffed themselves, I watched her tongue dart across her thin, dry lips and could tell she was suffering. That her body didn't need real food, couldn't even process it, didn't keep her mind from craving what everyone else was scarfing like a family of bears preparing to hibernate. (*Psychological needs*...I remembered.) Mom asked "Hugo, dear..." if she might have "...just a nibble?" Absolutely not. *Verboten.* But he soaked a washcloth in coffee, thick and sweet with cream, and let her suck on that.

I thought my moment had come when I remembered to tell Hugo about the electronic ping-pong game Mom's head and eyes had played the other night and how I'd rescued her. He produced a tiny jeweler's screwdriver, attacked Mom in the area of the jugular, and in a minute pronounced the problem "...*fixt!*" Nothing to it. After that, all the sisters were in love with him.

Nobody paid much attention to me.

It was dark by the time everyone, including Hugo, left. There still was plenty of food. I was in the kitchen discreetly romancing some crumb cake when I heard:

Click. Whirr.

"Son..."

I knew what was coming.

"Son...how about giving me a bite?"

"I'd love to, Mom," I answered with my mouth full, "but you heard what Hugo said."

"Sometimes Hugo can be a little too...fastidious. How could it hurt?"

"Mom, *you've got no guts!*"

"You're so crude..."

"No, really...think about it. If you eat, where's it going to go?"

"I can *taste* a bit, can't I? Put something – a piece of a meltaway or something – in my mouth and I'll just chew on it and spit it out...I promise."

MOM

"Yuk! You know that won't be satisfying. You'll probably gag..."

"You just don't want to make your mother happy."

"Look, I'll discuss it with Hugo, all right? I'm sure we're going to be seeing a lot of him..."

"You're jealous of Hugo..."

"Me? Why?"

"Because he's a better scientist than you are."

"I don't pretend to be a scientist..."

"And he's got a better way with women than you do."

"Aw, come on! That little dweeb?"

"You could learn a lot from him."

"I do okay—"

"Not with May..."

Mom knows how to hurt. But how could she know that I'd already fallen head over teakettle for May? I'd never met a woman quite like May, someone who could stand up for herself without being overbearing, someone so...together. Still, I couldn't entirely admit the strength of the attraction even to myself yet, much less to Mom. So I said:

"She's...not my type. Besides, you didn't let me finish. I do all right with women—"

"With a bunch of tramps, you mean."

"Will you let me finish? I do all right...*when I'm on my own.*"

"I knew it. You're not happy to have me back. I knew it..."

"Aw, Ma..." (Was she tearing up? Could she?)

"You don't love me...you don't love your own mother..."

"Of course I do, Mom. I love you."

"Then, if you love me...if you *really* love me – *give me a piece of cake!* Just a bite..."

"I...no, it's not me – you can't. *You can't!*"

"*Please, please, please, please, please...*"

"If only you came with an on-off switch..."

"I won't say anything more, if that's what you want."

Mom's silence for the rest of the evening was, as they say, deafening.

But when Monday morning came and May showed up you'd think we'd never argued. Mom even told May what a great help I'd been entertaining her sisters. I never can figure Mom. It didn't cut much ice with May, though. *Women!* Isn't another one supposed to be along in a minute, like public transportation? In my case the streetcar was named Lorna. Lorna and I had a heavy date on for Friday if her bowling team didn't make it into tournament finals. Scratch my itch and I'll scratch yours; that was how I'd always worked it with the opposite sex. That was the kind of relationship I had with Lorna. I've always liked women, liked them a lot, but I also like to keep them at a safe distance. I know what a dominatrix can be like (think Mom and her sisters). I'd had enough of involuntary servitude to not go and volunteer for it now, understanding the meaning of "lock" in wedlock only too well. No, it was going to be all my way, or "No way..."

Which probably is why I struck out so many times.

Over the next week, Hugo popped in almost as often as May, who remained the ice goddess as far as I was concerned. When Hugo and Mom weren't billing and cooing together, I got him to show me more about the support system. He tinkered to make Mom interactive, and soon there was no more channel changing for me. Mom also could phone her sisters by herself any time she wanted to. It really was ingenious, the way he rigged her up to control things remotely, with no hands, though it probably was natural for Mom, who'd been used to being in control – remote or otherwise – all the time anyway. Then it hit me: Mankind needed to learn about the breakthroughs achieved with Mom; in fact, Mankind was certain to be willing to shell out big bucks just to hear of it. Excited, I broached the matter with Hugo. Didn't he realize that with Mom we had a goose that could lay golden eggs? As a talking head, she was made for media. A couple more cable connections and Mom could have her own network.

"How about it?" I asked.

"We do not need *vulgar* publicity," he said. "In time," he pronounced loftily, "a tour of major medical and scientific centers is envisioned." It would be highly professional, though, and very academic; such monetary gains as might accrue would "of course" go to the Institute. (*Of course*...) That was the deal Mom had cut with them in exchange for a perpetual care package a pharaoh would've envied.

Damn! Maybe I ought to write a book...

At least I still had pleasures of the flesh to look forward to. Lorna needed serious consoling after her bowling club bombed in the tournament. On Friday night, I sprung for a big feed for the two of us at a Chinese restaurant where I figured I got her oiled enough on mai-tai's (her favorite drink) to face Mom with equanimity. We had to come back to the house; Mom and Lorna weren't what anybody would

MOM

call friends, but Lorna's big family prevented us from doing anything at her parents' place, where she lived. And she always felt a motel room was for sluts. I was planning to try our old routine of saying a quick "Hi – Bye!" to Mom and then run off to the bedroom for a well-deserved piece of paradise behind closed doors.

Lorna wobbled into the front room on my strong arm. I thought I'd prepared her for what to expect. Not quite. Mom had found a way to toss off her wig. She had the TV mute and the room in darkness (she was in control of the lights now, too) except for a single spot that illuminated her from below to diabolical effect. Her unblinking eyes glittered like the pendulous earrings which, on that bald head, gave her the look of a pagan idol. Lorna came from a superstitious background and was squeamish about the paranormal. I'd forgotten how "para" Mom was.

With her eyes getting about the size of the headlights on a car, all Lorna could manage was "...uh, *hi!* Mrs. Kravath," giving a nervous little wave of one hand as she clutched her stomach with the other. *Uh-oh.* All that cheap Chinese food, I told myself.

Click. Whirr.

"Hello...Lorna..." Mom pronounced in her best space-to-earth monotone.

Click. Whirr.

"What's that?" Lorna said, "What's that sound? That...click?"

"Oh, *that*...that's nothing." I tried to sound reassuring. "Just Mom's speaking apparatus going on and off. That's how she talks. I told you about it...remember?"

"*Jeez...*"

Click. Whirr.

"I guess Mom doesn't have anything else to say...must be tired. G'night, Mom. C'mon, Lorna..."

Lorna whispered behind her hand: "It's kinda *creepy*..."

As we scuttled across the floor, she wouldn't turn her back on Mom, who rotated to track our movement. It felt as if we were being locked onto by hostile radar. But we made it out of sight, and I breathed a sigh of relief – too soon.

"I think I'm gonna be sick..."

Lorna spent ten minutes in the bathroom. I have to admit she looked a lot better when she came out. More sober, too, so I figured it probably was just as well. After the briefest of preliminaries, we were undressed and in bed. Soon we were getting it on, as usual.

MOM

"All those weeks...didja miss me, baby?"
"Yeah..."
"I missed you, too. Mmm..."
Then she sat bolt upright.
"Wha-what'sa matter?" I asked.
"Listen..."
"I don't hear anything."
"It's too quiet. Your Mother always plays the TV when we're in here."
"She must be real tired tonight. She's been through a lot, y'know...dying and losing her body and coming back an' all..."
"I think she's listening to us."

It took quite a while and all my powers of persuasion to b.s. Lorna about Mom's hearing not being what it used to be. (Mom actually could hear a flea scratching itself anywhere in the house now, thanks to the Eterna Institute!) Anyway, Lorna finally swallowed my story and we got back to where we'd been before *coitus* was so rudely *interruptus* by Mom's silence. We were getting into it again when—

Click. Whirr.
"What's that?"
"You know," I said, "It's Mom's speaking thingamajig again."
Click. Whirr.
"Why's she turning it on and off like that?"

"I don't know…"

Click. Whirr.

"Maybe she needs something. Go see…"

I pulled on a bathrobe and stuck my head into the front room. I didn't like the way the evening was progressing at all.

"Need anything, Ma?" I asked in a booming voice so Lorna would be sure to hear.

Silencio.

Back to bed again. No time to get into the groove before—

Click. Whirr.

"That…*noise*," said Lorna, "that strange noise…I can't do anything with that noise all the time."

"Click, whirr" was all she could think about now.

Lorna wouldn't go to a motel, her parents' house was out of the question, and it was too cold outside to fool around in the car. I even thought of my workshop, but it's far away and the heat isn't on at night.

"I'm sorry…" she said.

What really made me mad was having to walk by Mom (no other way out of the house) with her so smugly quiet, eyes shut, a smile that could have been the face of gloating victory frozen on her lips. Before we were out the door she gave one last, triumphant—

Click. Whirr.

Guess I did get screwed that night after all...

When I got back from taking Lorna home the Temple of Gloom lighting was gone and Mom was watching TV, as usual, looking as "normal" as she could. Out of spite, I didn't replace her wig. Still, she was unruffled.

"I never liked that girl," she said, "You can do a lot better."

I noticed there wasn't the "click, whirr" any more.

"Son..."

"Yeah?"

"Give me a cigarette."

At one time, Mom had smoked like a fifties TV commercial. Cigarettes were what killed her.

"You haven't smoked for over a year and a half. You haven't got any cigarettes."

"I know where some are..."

"Don't they go stale or something?"

I didn't know whether I went along with her because I was beginning to think it was pointless to go against Mom's wishes or because I hoped the cigarettes would be bad for her and teach her a lesson. The coffin nails were just where she said they would be. How could she remember something like that? I helped her light up and put an ashtray on her shoulder – on top of the black box, that is – so she could turn and flick the ash when she needed to. Bobbing up and down, for some reason she reminded me of a parrot on its perch.

"Maybe Hugo can hook up something like a car cigarette lighter for you," I said.

"Don't you tell him about this."

Soon Mom was puffing away like an infernal engine. Clamping down fiercely to keep the butt from falling from her lips, surrounding herself with smoke, she savored the taste of the weed that'd made her what she was: dead. Or was it more accurate now to call her "undead?" Well, I figured she didn't have many pleasures left. At the thought of how Lorna would've reacted to the sight, I had to laugh out loud. It'd been a long, long night.

I fell asleep in the chair.

The next time Hugo came to visit, I brought up the question of food, as I'd told Mom I would. I thought of the gesture mostly as a peace offering; if I at least asked, maybe she wouldn't be so rough on me. But I was beginning seriously to wonder if there was a way she might be able to taste a little.

"Couldn't we fix it so something fairly liquid" – soup or gelatine or ice cream (Mom loved ice cream) – "would...uh, pass *through* her?"

"It would be of no nutritional value," said Hugo. "She does not need –"

"She needs it *psychologically...*" I interjected, replaying what May had told me. "Besides, it'll please her. You want to make her happy, don't you?"

Hugo saw my point; he'd do anything to make Mom happy. I suggested we cut Mom's throat. Hugo gasped as I hurried to explain what I meant:

"We could put an exit chute below her epiglottis – if she still has one. There already are tubes to carry away the moisture that keeps her mouth from drying out. Why not something a bit larger? Sure, it would be a little messy...*like the messy machinery of the body,*" I was pleased to observe. "Then she could enjoy all the sensations of tasting and swallowing."

After silently considering my suggestions for several minutes (probably working logarithmic equations in his head) Hugo's face lit up like some iGizmo app and he declared: "It *can* be done!" He sputtered that we simultaneously could boost the glucose level in the brain to make Mom feel satisfied.

"Now you're talking," I said, "Fat and happy again, with all of Baskin and Robbins' hundred and something flavors to choose from!"

Long into the night we labored. We did the work ourselves – Hugo and I – with plastic tubing, wire, and clamps. Hugo looked like a cross between a surgeon, embalmer, and plumbing contractor, more the mad scientist than ever. I shudder to think what I, as stoked as he was by then, must've been like. We certainly had to be a pair! I found out Hugo wasn't just a theoretician; he was good with his hands, good with tools. I respect that. We worked well together. He wasn't a bad guy at all.

And *voila!* Before she went to bed (figuratively speaking), Mom was able to eat a dish of ice cream (again, figuratively speaking). Her pleasure knew no bounds. I got a kick out of seeing her so happy, the "Empress of Ice Cream." She never was this easy to please before death and decapitation. Hugo, smiling, took his leave.

Then Mom and I were alone. I figured it was as good a time as any to bring up something

MOM

that had been on my mind. I tried my best to be casual about it:

"Uh, Mom...what do you and May talk about all day long?" I asked. "You know...when you're alone together, just the two of you? When I'm not here?"

"Nothing special...girl stuff mostly."

That was not the information I was looking for. I went on:

"Does she ever mention anything about...me?"

"Sometimes. Why do you want to know?"

Mom knew full well why. It had never been easy for me to be direct with her about personal matters, but I persisted:

"Just wanted to find out...if I even have a chance..."

"With May? Of course you do. If you do it right."

"Well, I never see any sign she's thawing..."

"That's 'cause you don't do it right."

"What do you mean?"

Now I'd gone and asked her for advice. Mom normally would use an opening like that to her advantage, like a wrestler discovering a hidden weakness in an opponent. But I thought this time she really wanted to help.

"When you talk with May it always sounds too much as if you're handing her a pickup line," Mom said. "A lame one, too. You've got to get beyond that."

"And do what?"

"Just be yourself. And be *nice*...though maybe that's not being yourself, exactly."

Mom never quite lets me forget where I get my penchant for zingers. Still, she continued:

"Let May know you like her."

"She should have that figured out by now. What more can I do?"

"Tell her, for god's sake...in a *nice* way. And show her, too."

"But what if it falls flat?"

"Then try, try, try again. It works, y'know. Believe me, I'm speaking from experience..."

Maybe, but I wasn't so sure – of myself.

The next day, Mom couldn't stop telling May about what I'd accomplished: making it possible for her to "eat," praising me for it. It was all my idea, she said, my engineering. You would've thought I'd given her a Playboy Bunny body transplant or something. Of course, she went on, it wasn't surprising I should be so smart, since I'd undoubtedly gotten my brains from her. But I was being *"so considerate..."* too.

MOM

"Don't you think, dear?" she pointedly asked May.

May raised her eyebrows maybe a quarter of an inch. Was she impressed?

She hadn't seen anything yet. I had ideas. BIG ideas.

I was going to make Mom even more hell on wheels than she already was. Literally. Early on, Hugo had said Mom was transportable; I was planning to build a dolly that would make it possible for her to be moved around easily. Then I'd be able to get her out of the house for a while. Mom always used to like riding in the car, going nowhere in particular, seeing what was happening in our part of the world. April was certain to bring better weather; if I could move her, I could take her out for rides then. It would do wonders to improve her mood, and elevating Mom's mood was a high priority for me. I had to live with her. It might make May think a little better of me, too. Besides, it gave me a reason to get back to my workshop again. I rechecked the technical aspects of moving Mom with Hugo, and he concurred with my plans. He called the dolly I was proposing a "transporter."

Why use two syllables when three will do?

It wasn't a big deal, really, just one of those simple, two-wheeled things that everyone has used at one time or another to move boxes — with handles up high in back and a little shelf out in front of a single axle. Slide it under the load (Mom's portable black box support module in this case), tilt backward a little, and wheel away. Reverse procedure to unload. Not comfortable for long distances but adequate to go from house to car. Then I could lift Mom onto the seat and belt her in. They brought her into the house using a dolly something like this. But mine was a lot better. I built mine out of gleaming chrome gussied up with multicolored bungee cords to hold the module securely, and I used inflatable tires for a soft ride. I even decked it out in ribbons and streamers for the maiden voyage.

She *loved* it! Ensconced in the front seat (which I'd lowered), the torso-sized black box that was Mom's "body" was hard to spot from outside the car. Her head, looking reasonably normal, was all anyone could see unless they got up close and stuck their own head in the window.

I wasn't about to let *that* happen.

III

THE CHANCE TO LEAVE THE HOUSE AT WILL, to be out and about again, quickly became something Mom couldn't resist, and she never was in any hurry to return home when we went for a ride. I figured the four-hour time limit of the portable support system would be more than enough for our orbit. I didn't mind carting Mom around, either; it sure was better than staying in the house with her. Everything worked fine except I thought the transporter a little primitive for negotiating terrain. Already I was mentally preoccupied with designing a new and improved version. We ranged farther and farther afield, just the two of us, sometimes stopping to buy ice cream or surprising one of the aunts for a short visit. Mom and I even began to get bold about maxing out the support module's allotted time. It wouldn't be a big tragedy, I thought, if we overstayed the limit and the black box began to shut her down; she could always be revived simply by reconnecting back at the house. Simply – that's what Hugo had said

One day we dawdled until it started to rain – hard. Still plenty of time to make it home. Then I got a flat. It was quite a job to change a tire in the downpour, especially since an eight-hundred-pound gorilla must've tightened the lug nuts. I needed to jump up and down on the handle of the wrench to break those babies free, and I figured the greater part of the four hours had to be up by the time I got done. Soaked through to the skin, sitting in a wet spot that probably was ruining my upholstery, I put the pedal to the metal to speed away. I guess I made a rolling stop through an empty four-way intersection. The "moving violation" was not missed by a cop lying in classic wait behind a billboard.

A ticket. So what? So long as it didn't take too much time. We weren't far from home now. I thought the only thing I had to worry about was whether Mom would fall in love with the "bubblegum machine" on top of the patrol car (*heh*). But I knew I was in trouble the way the cop, with his big donut shop gut, took his sweet time sauntering over to my car – as if he'd reserved the rest of the day just to make me suffer. You'd have thought he'd want to hurry things along so he could get out of the rain. But *no-o*. He had to be a Nazi, to play cat and

MOM

mouse. He stuck his head in the driver's side window and drawled:

"Didn't you see the stop sign...*sir?*

He said "sir" the way most people would say "...*scumbag.*"

"Yes, officer..."

"Why didn't you stop then?"

"I...don't know, officer..."

"You don't know?"

"I mean...I *thought* I stopped..."

"You don't know whether you stopped or not? You driving impaired...*sir?*"

"No...*sir.*"

All the while, I was counting myself lucky the dufus hadn't noticed anything strange about my having a legless companion sealed in a black box with only her head showing. Wow, I thought, cops really do get used to just about *everything.* Then I got it – he didn't know Mom was for real, probably figured she was some kind of display mannequin, maybe from a makeup counter.

"Please, Mom..." I prayed silently, *"Please don't say anything."*

But that isn't her way. She swiveled around like a naval gun and let him have it broadside: *"You asshole!"*

"Wha'...wha'd you say?"

I hadn't said a thing.

"Why don't you just write the ticket and let us get the hell out of here?" It was Mom talking. "We're in a hurry!"

"What the hell's *that?*" the cop said, gawking for the first time at Mom. Then to me: *"You!* Outta the car." He even drew his revolver.

I did as ordered. In the rain again, I went over to the patrol car. I hadn't gotten any drier since changing the tire but, driving with the heater on, at least I was beginning to feel a little warmer. There was no heat in the cop car, the windows were cracked open, and every time the radio squawked it made me jump. Each bit of information I provided had to be checked out with headquarters at great pains to make sure I wasn't a terrorist or an escaped ax murderer or something. It took a long time.

"Besides the moving violation, I'm gonna write you up for interfering with a law officer acting in the line of duty. Whatta ya got to say to that, wise ass?"

I'd taken enough of his crap by then and just had to turn the tables.

"I'm sorry," I said, "I couldn't resist doing what I did back there...with Mom, my *dummy*..."

I paused to let it sink in. I knew this guy needed time.

MOM

"That's what I call my dummy," I said "...*Mom.*"

Still nothing. Did I have to write it down for him?

"Think of it," I said. "It'll make a great story. Network TV, millions of viewers, the whole country watching. And me telling the world how you did your duty..."

"Huh?"

"I'm a ventriloquist...and I'm going to be on late-night TV tonight." I dropped the name of one of the shows Mom liked to watch and tried again, spelling it out:

"That's my dummy...for the act. On TV..."

"*Yeah?*" (Finally!)

"What's *your* name, officer?"

"Sergeant James Doan, sir..." ("sir" pronounced with due civility this time).

"Tomorrow morning, Sgt. James Doan will be a household word...for an officer who did his duty, even in a rainstorm. It's a human interest kind of story. Good publicity for the force. Won't hurt toward helping you make lieutenant, either, I'll bet."

"No shit?"

"I promise."

"I still have to cite you for running the stop sign...to show I'm doing my duty..."

"I understand."

He ambled back to my car with me, shaking my hand, asking my stage name. I made up something, told him it was a new act. He asked more stupid questions. Didn't he *ever* want to get out of the rain? Again I prayed Mom would find the good grace to keep quiet, and this time – thank God – she just stared ahead blankly.

I could tell the fat cop's mind was working on something, though. At last, he said:

"Don't you think it'd be ah…better if I appeared on the show…with you?"

"Well…yes, sure." I gulped. I had to think fast. "But with a ticket pending, there might be a legal problem. A conflict of interest thing…"

He thought a minute more, then said, "*Aw*…what the hell…" and made a big deal of tearing the ticket into tiny pieces.

"You'll be getting a call from the producer," I told him. "Better yet, call this number as soon as you get off duty." I scribbled a phone number on a piece of paper. "Ask for Mr. Wolfe." (I gave him the Bronx Zoo.)

Victory was sweet.

"That was a close one…" I said to Mom as we drove away at precisely 24 miles per hour. I'd lost all track of time by then, so I asked, "How many minutes do we have left, Mom?"

MOM

"Mom?"

No answer. I looked over at her. Mom never sat motionless and unblinking, not to mention speechless, in the car. I reached across and rapped playfully on the black box to rouse her (she *hated* that).

Nothing. I almost went off the road.

She'd started cycling into shut-down mode, involuntarily. Mom didn't like doing anything involuntarily. Besides the silence and lack of movement, her color was changing. She looked the way she did when she first came into the house: waxy, bloodless...*lifeless*. My hands began to get clammy on the wheel and I started to drive real fast again. I tried to tell myself this was the way it was supposed to happen, that I knew what to do, how to recharge her once we got home. But I couldn't help feeling it was an emergency. I'd never let it happen before.

To move things along I left the dolly behind and carried Mom bodily into the house in my arms. The module was pretty heavy but I was adrenalized. Her head got wet in the rain, and I worried the water might short her out. My face was wet now, too, with tears. I wasted no time reconnecting to the main support system. May wasn't there; when Mom and I went out in the afternoon I usually let her take the rest of the day off. Now I knew that was a mistake. I tried to phone, but May wasn't home. I didn't want to be alone at a time like this, so I called the Institute to speak with Hugo, as much for moral support as anything. He meant to reassure me by saying, "You *haf* simply to wait..." But he hadn't been there, hadn't seen it happening. He didn't have himself to blame.

I hung up and stood over Mom. Talk about a watched pot that never boils! I wondered whether I ought to say a prayer or something. After half an hour on full power, Mom's eyelids started to flutter. She looked around as if trying to get her bearings. Her lips moved soundlessly before she could say anything.

"Mom!" I cried, and hugged the black box. *"You're back!"*

"Don't let that happen again..." were the first words she uttered, more shaken up than mad at me. "Don't *ever* let that happen."

"I won't, Mom, I promise..." In tears, I kissed her.

"I *hate* that...going comatose." She, too, was sobbing (electromechanically). "It's so much like...like *death*—all over again."

Death.

MOM

"Mom...can you tell me now? What was it like...to die? Can you share it with me? You know how much it would mean to me..."

Silence.

"Just tell me...if it's anything like what they say." That was all I wanted to know.

Mom gave a snort of resignation and said:

"Well, first you feel you're floating or flying, like a bird. Then there's this light...far, far away, drawing you. You hear music...except it's not a tune or anything, just sort of humming. But pretty. You rise up high enough to look down on everybody...and feel sorry – *for them!* You have a sense of peace, tranquility, beauty..."

I was so moved. "It's *true*, then..."

I thought Mom's eyes rolled. Was there a malfunction somewhere? She couldn't keep it up:

"It's a load of crap..."

"Huh...What's that, Ma?"

"I said, 'It's a load of crap!' I got all that from a talk show. You'd believe anything. That's why you need somebody to take care of you..."

I stepped back.

"The part about feeling light-headed and calm is true...that's *before* you die. After, it's nothingness! Nothing is all I ever felt, anyway. That's why I hate it so much. Maybe it gets better later on...angels and pearly gates and such. Maybe it's worse. I don't know. Probably takes time to reach wherever you're going. I don't mean to find out just yet."

She did her best *"Dark Victory"* turn:

"*I want to live...*"

No more was said about it.

But, for a week, Mom couldn't stop telling May about how I'd "saved" her. She went over every detail of what I'd done as if it'd been something great – fixing the flat in the rain, driving fast to try to get home, flummoxing the obnoxious cop, carrying her into the house in my arms...*crying*. May couldn't have been more clued-in to what happened if she'd been there. Mom didn't even carp that it'd been my fault in the first place. She made me out to be a hero, a hero with a heart. It almost was a little embarrassing. I hoped at last May might start to see me in a better light.

Not long after that, Mom confided in me:

"May likes you. I only wish you two can be as happy one day as Hugo and I are..."

I had to crack, "You and Hugo, huh? You mean, like...I should *lose my head* over her?"

"Asshole..."

MOM

But each of us knew what the other was trying to say.

Mom had never been like this before. While she'd always complained that I ought to be going out with "good" girls, she never pushed me toward any one in particular. Couldn't she tell that with May I didn't need to be pushed? I was there already. That didn't mean May had fallen for *me*, though.

I figured Mom's interest in love had to be because of the ever-blooming romance between her and Hugo. I don't know much about what her feelings had been for my father; he died while I was an infant, a time that still was hard for Mom to talk about. But with Hugo you couldn't fail to see it was the real thing. He seemed to be around more and more now, after working hours, of course. And he always brought flowers. I would find him in the front room slurping coffee with Mom at the oddest times, the two of them whispering together, oblivious to anyone else. All they needed was each other.

Yet Hugo gave Mom more; he gave her – The World! He put her in complete control of every home entertainment device known to man and, when she tired of those, she could manipulate the surveillance cameras he set up outside around the house to spy on the street, viewing all the drama of real life better than she could have managed with the unassisted eye. He gave her internet access, of course, with a virtual identity to hide her true persona, although she was able to switch to a computer camera when talking with her sisters. (I wonder if she ever got mixed up.) Mom had an e-reader and could play games, too. In fact, she's naturally good at computer games since she doesn't have to contend with hand-eye coordination issues. Mom didn't lack things to do even when Hugo wasn't there.

Still, with spring, the weather was beginning to get nicer and, despite our big misadventure, Mom continued to enjoy going out. I'd learned from my mistakes. In my workshop, I fabricated a set of independently sprung, small diameter wheels that I fixed permanently in place beneath the life support module (the black box). This new "traction unit," as I called it with Hugo's approval, looked like the undercarriage of a big cargo plane. I couldn't resist including power so Mom could get around by herself a little – slowly, the way a lunar lander moves. The traction unit wasn't meant for long distances or to negotiate a grade (not enough *oomph*) but would be useful in case of emergency. If there should be a fire or something when she was alone, Mom could disconnect from the equipment in the basement and roll herself to safety. She'd be able to move over a variety of surfaces or lock in place, even on a slight incline, with a brake. It would do wonders for her sense of autonomy.

I was especially proud of the stability of the device. Although it made her a little "taller," it was totally balanced, rendering Mom almost impossible to tip over, and it always ran straight and true, with no tendency to swerve or crash, even when rolling free. Hugo and I tested the "hot wheels" (Mom's name for the unit) on a mock-up of the black box for stability at speeds far in excess of anything she should experience unless she enters a soapbox derby. They worked perfectly every time. Like fabrication, the testing had to be conducted at my workshop where I had the equipment, not to mention space, to do it. Hugo accompanied me out there; we were chums by then, and I enjoyed showing him around the place.

I'd reconfigured the workshop out of what'd originally been an independent auto repair facility. There still was a working lift. In fact, I'd started out as an automotive engineer myself and enjoyed some real success in that line. But redesigning the guts of a motor, no matter how remunerative, just wasn't fun after a while. Not enough human interaction, not enough novelty. I preferred the more creative kinds of products found in the mail order world. Hugo didn't think that was so odd. When it comes to odd, though, what *could* he think? Anyway, we worked really well together again. And he was impressed with my workshop.

Even with the traction unit, I continued to have to supply some manpower to get Mom into and out of the car. I also realized, after what happened the day she "died" on the road, that it'd be wise always to have another person along. May was happy to come with us, riding in the front seat beside me. Mom insisted on sitting by herself in back, said she was able to see fine and liked being in the middle. I'd taken the rear seat out so she could be braced securely over the center hump. That made more room for air to circulate. With all the electronics in the support module, it was sure to heat up as the weather got warmer. The car had air conditioning, but I was afraid it might not be adequate to take care of all Mom's equipment. As we drove along, I kept an eye on her in the rear-view mirror.

MOM

We scouted for places where we could stop and let her out for an airing and "attitude adjustment" (read: cool down) without attracting attention. Although Mom probably could've survived on Venus – her parameters for safety being much broader than for comfort – I knew she would be happiest in the same temperate zone she'd preferred all her life. She wasn't a hot weather person and, as I never tired of stressing to May, "It's a *psychological* thing…" (I'd learned that much by heart.) We found small, secluded parks that didn't have a lot of public in the middle of the week, perfect places to let Mom go and roll around. It was good for her circuitry, and it gave May and me a chance to stretch our legs. The best stops were along the shoreline; the month of April was early for the vacation crowd, but the view and the sea air were invigorating. Roses seemed to bloom in Mom's cheeks. The relaxed, day-off-from-school atmosphere and the intimacy of riding in the car together for hours worked magic on May's mood as well.

I felt I still needed something more to help me get it on with her, though. What Mom had said about telling May how I felt about her probably was the right thing to do – in theory. But I doubted I could put it over, not the way I wanted to come across. Maybe it was too important to me. I wanted to *impress* her. What to do then? Hugo had been impressed with my workshop, and he's no fool; I figured showing off the shop was my best way to wow May, too. I sneaked off to clean and straighten and polish the place until it gleamed like a yacht. You could almost eat off the floor by the time I was done. I was proud of it. My thinking was to "just stop by" there – casually – when we all were out for a ride, on the pretext that I had to pick up a part I needed for Mom's traction unit, a replacement wheel or something. It couldn't be a long visit because Mom had been out plenty of times before and never was that interested in valves and gauges (although now I didn't know; with her support system in the basement, the place might seem more like home to her). At any rate, May would get to have a look around and be impressed. I was counting on that.

    I decided I'd better run the idea of a stop by the shop past Mom first. If she was set against going on a given day for some reason, it might be a problem to repeat the ploy any time soon, and I could keep the place spotless only so long. I wasn't too worried because Mom loved going for a ride so much she never balked. She would

MOM

set off in a blizzard if I suggested it. A little diversion to the workshop shouldn't be a problem then. Imagine my surprise when she said she didn't feel like going out *at all* that day! But she didn't want to stop May and me from going. (*Whew*...) In fact, she made a big point of insisting in front of May that we go together without her. Mom explained she needed some afternoon "quiet time" by herself.

"I *vant* to be alone..." she emoted.

While this was a new one as far as Mom was concerned, it was more than I'd dared to dream of: May and me together...by ourselves. If May bought it, that is. And she did!

Driving out, I knew enough to shut up and let May talk about herself (I'm not a complete klutz when it comes to women). I learned she's a Midwestern girl, come east to experience the bright lights and sophistication of our "old world." Her hometown in Nebraska is in the heart of farm country. I could almost see the sign announcing "Pop. 7,500" on the edge of town, out by where the corn stands rustling in the wind. It turns out she has two older brothers and a younger sister, lots of uncles and aunts and cousins, but only one maiden aunt who, I understood, still had hope. In other words, a normal family. That seemed wildly exotic to me. May's mother was a homemaker, and her father sold and serviced farm machinery – the big stuff, harvesters and combines. Both her brothers were motorheads, the kind of kids who'd built their own tractor – from the wheels up – as a Four H project in junior high. I worried that might throw a monkey wrench into the works. May probably had enough of things mechanical, maybe *too* much, all her life. And my little operation could seem small potatoes by comparison.

I pressed on regardless. It wasn't so bad once we got to the workshop. May appreciated my stuff more than most women would. She knew what everything was (Mom never had) and asked intelligent questions. I'd meant for May to be impressed; as it turned out, *she* impressed *me*. But she certainly thought my place was impressively clean and neat. She asked if I actually did any work there, knowing from experience how messy a "real" workshop gets.

"Or," she went on with a smile in her voice, "maybe you just keep it like this to impress all your girlfriends?"

"Oh, no," I answered quickly, "I've never shown the workshop to any women before – other than Mom, that is. Not just anyone could

MOM

understand what it means to me." Hugo's a guy, and an engineer, too, so he doesn't count.

May got kind of quiet as she looked around some more. Then, the practical side of her coming out, she asked:

"But how do you make a living here...from inventing, I mean?"

For a fleeting moment I thought it was time to show her the prototype portable bidet that was sure to make a million, but I thought better of it. I decided to come clean.

"Well...I don't really need the money; not a lot of money, anyway. You see, when I started out, straight from college I designed a major modification for automotive engine induction systems. Basically, it lets you go farther faster on less gas. The Big Three automakers all picked it up, and I get a regular royalty check that pretty much pays the bills. It's not so much money that I can afford to do nothing, but enough so I can do something I really love. I lost interest in working on stuff that hides out of sight. I like to think my inventions make real people smile...and maybe laugh sometimes. Call me crazy, but that's important to me. I guess I could always go back and start on my first billion..."

"No...no, I understand..." was all May said.

I didn't know if I came anywhere close to hitting the mark. I only knew I'd taken my best shot.

After a while, as we were driving home to Mom, May asked, "Why do you pretend to be so cynical all the time? To hide behind a wise guy mask?"

I had to think carefully (didn't want to blow it now). I decided to be honest again and said, "To be...tough, I guess."

"Are you afraid to show your feelings?"

"Dad died before I could know him. I grew up an only child surrounded by Mom and four maiden aunts. Sometimes, I'm not sure how I'm *supposed* to feel. Or act. So, to be on the safe side, to be...a man, I guess I overcompensate."

"I think you're more sensitive than you like to let on..."

A good sign? I wondered.

One sign that couldn't be questioned was the promise of the coming summer. Though real summer still was weeks away, it soon was the month May had been named for, and the weather stirred something in Mom's synthetic blood as inexorable as the will of a mallard to migrate. The need to ramble had been considerable even when grey skies predominated. Now each bright morning

MOM

beckoned with all the fresh excitement of the first day after school lets out. Maybe every new day really is a gift to someone who's gone through as much as Mom had. On our rides, she especially liked to have me stop and park so she could get out and roll around all by herself. Ambulatory self-sufficiency was a real novelty for her. That traction unit was turning out to be the best thing I'd ever put together. While Mom was perambulating it gave me time alone with May, too. Still, it taxed our imagination to find places for Mom to take the air without risking the kind of attention that an unplanned landing by a passing blimp might attract.

Our favorite spot was by a sailors' cenotaph half hidden in a stand of trees at the top of a long hill overlooking the water. For a place with such a great view, it was pretty secluded; a road that led straight up from a precipitous seawall to the memorial had been closed to vehicular traffic for years and was enough of an uphill climb that few people walked it. Everyone preferred to sit on the benches at the bottom of the hill where they could look out to sea, watching waves crash at the base of the seawall. But we discovered a quiet street up the hill on the back side where we could park and move Mom by a little-used gate to the cenotaph.

There we would be completely unnoticed by anyone below. May had knitted a light cover that looked like a shawl to put over Mom's black box. If someone did chance to glance our way, at a distance Mom simply would appear to be a person in a wheelchair. As I said, it was a great vantage point, way up high. There, in a spirit of fun, May and I competed to see which of us could spot the first sailboats of the season as they appeared on the horizon.

One day, maybe we got too absorbed in this game, and in each other. I turned around and Mom was gone. It didn't take more than a second to see what was happening. She was rolling down the hill! She must've tried to change position and gone off the level ground where we left her. Then gravity took over. The road down to the seawall was inclined like a ski jump. It totally exceeded the design limits for the brakes on the traction unit. *Why hadn't Mom yelled for help?* She didn't have much of a lead yet but already was beyond stopping or even slowing herself, and she was gaining speed – fast!

I started to sprint after her. I'm not built for running – nobody in my family is – and it's surprisingly hard to run downhill. Still, propelled by nothing less than sheer terror, I

MOM

was bettering my personal best that day. May could've passed me easily most times, but I *had* to catch up with Mom. So I really poured it on. There wasn't anything to stop Mom before she slammed into a granite barrier less than two feet high atop the seawall. The physics of the worst case scenario were obvious: when it hit that barrier Mom's support module would smash and what was left of it – and of her – would topple over into the sea.

I *couldn't* let that happen. I didn't like it when the hot wheels started to smoke. That meant the brakes were losing what little effect they had. (I admit I spent a nanosecond noting how stable the module remained on my undercarriage, though.) But I still had plenty to worry about. I wondered what I could do even if I caught up, how I could safely grab the module and stop its descent. I studied the lay of the land. The road we were racing down formed a "T" intersection with another, wider thoroughfare that followed along the seawall. If I got out ahead, I could cross that road first and put myself between Mom and the stone barrier that was the only thing separating her from oblivion. If I didn't at least deflect her, it was *crash!* and into the water for sure.

I doubted the black box was immersible like an electric skillet. Even if it was, its watertight integrity would be compromised on impact with the barrier. Would the batteries in the box explode on contact with seawater? I conjured a horrific image of Mom and everything that was keeping her alive being blown to smithereens.

Speed...I had to have more speed!

I put my head down and dug in. Out of the corner of an eye, I saw I was pulling even with Mom. I heard a heart-stopping thump when she hit the intersection, but the traction unit's wheels kept her steady. (Good design; I found myself wishing Hugo could be there to see how well it performed.) Coming off the incline as she crossed the intersection, Mom slowed just enough for me to get out ahead, then position myself between her and the stone barrier above the precipice. I hardly had time to spin around. Slipping, my back to the barrier, I raised my hands to try to give her a shunt.

WHOMP! I hadn't anticipated the force with which she would strike. Mom did more than knock the wind out of me. I blacked out. The last thing I remember was the sensation of going over the barrier – over the seawall – with her in my arms.

Then falling...*falling...*

MOM

I never felt myself hit the water, never thought I was drowning, or even wet. It was as if we'd transitioned into another world, another plane of existence, sinking together in slow motion. Were we both dead? Is *this* what death is like? Being weightless in a warm, green sea? Why was the water so warm this time of year?

Full fathom five thy mother lies...

"Mom! Mom!" I heard myself crying.

I came to my senses in May's arms. She was wiping my forehead as I sat by the roadside. The sound of waves crashing against the seawall, the rough granite barrier digging into my back, provided a reality check. Mom was in the road, rolling back and forth, doing an excellent job holding at bay a small group of curious onlookers who had gathered, naturally attracted by the commotion.

"Back! Keep back! Give him air...give 'im room to breathe!" she commanded.

The first thing I remember was feeling pleased the traction unit still worked.

May was fighting back tears, saying something about *"How brave!"* I'd been. She hugged me and kept trying to clean me up. Mom stayed apart but looked our way often. Even bleary-eyed and with my "bell rung" badly, I knew she winked at me. Only then did I fully realize I'd stopped her, that we hadn't gone over the top at all. Thank God. May didn't want to leave me to get the car, but it was parked pretty far away and I wasn't up to climbing that hill. She wanted to call a doctor for me.

"I'm okay...I'm okay..." I insisted, wondering whether I truly was.

I didn't hear all of what she said then, only the words "...*tough guy.*" But she was smiling.

I asked her gently, "Get the car. Please..."

After she left, I turned to Mom. I had to know:

"Did you do that – go down the hill...on purpose?"

"I thought you were faster on your feet, son..."

"Why would you do such a crazy thing?"

"You and May needed a push...to get together."

"I'd say that was a pretty risky shove."

"You've got to have somebody who cares about you...everybody does."

Though May had headed off at a good clip, it was impossible for her to come back with the car before one of the gawkers called the police. They arrived along with a news team that snapped a couple of photos of May and me and about a hundred, plus video, of Mom. We

MOM

avoided a lot of questions by promising, after getting Mom's consent, to hold a press conference in the morning. As soon as we arrived home, we called Hugo to alert him to watch for us on the five o'clock news, with film at eleven. He said he'd come right over "to plan the strategy" now that Mom's privacy had been breached.

I was worried about this far more than either of them, as it turned out. They'd been intending to "go public" soon; here was a dramatic way to break the news. At the press conference the next day, in addition to answering questions about the scientific and medical breakthroughs represented by what he cautiously characterized only as Mom's "return," Hugo took the opportunity to announce their upcoming speaking tour together. But first, Mom declared to the world, they were going to be married! A June wedding. She explained privately to me she felt free to go ahead now that I was on the right track with May. She claimed:

"I don't need to take care of you all by myself any more..."

She had been taking care of *me*?

With Hugo beaming by her side, Mom said that after the tour the two of them were going to live at the Institute, where she'd serve as resident advisor to people seeking prostheses. She's uniquely qualified, I guess, since she has the ultimate prosthesis. Mom made me promise to visit. Since she was completely mobile now – *"Thanks to you, son"* – she said she'd come see me, too. I could live in the house on Oak Street, if I wanted to, for free, as long as I wished. Mom hoped May and I would.

"Don't you think you're rushing things a bit," I said, "as far as my future with May is concerned?"

"A mother knows these things…"

Maybe she's right. May had gotten the two of us tickets to an inventors' exposition in New York that afternoon that I really wanted to attend. In fact, it already was time for me to go pick her up.

I kissed Mom good-bye. I had to leave her then.

STEPHEN ZACK is a Connecticut shoreline native. A graduate of Yale and Cornell, he served the U.S. Government for thirty years as an Intelligence Officer.

Made in the USA
Lexington, KY
13 December 2012